A cut above the NORMAL

AF669472

A cut above the NORMAL

Dr. A.P. Maheshwari

PRABHAT PRAKASHAN

No part of this publication can be reproduced, stored in a retrieval system or transmitted in any form or by any means, electronic, mechanical, photocopying, recording or otherwise, without the prior permission of the author and the publisher.

Published by
PRABHAT PRAKASHAN PVT. LTD.
4/19 Asaf Ali Road,
New Delhi-110 002 (INDIA)
e-mail: prabhatbooks@gmail.com

ISBN 978-93-90923-93-9
***A cut above the* NORMAL**
by Dr. A.P. Maheshwari

© Reserved

Edition
2025

Price
₹ 300.00 (Rupees Three Hundred only)

Printed at
R-Tech Offset Printers, Delhi

Initiation

Life is like an ocean voyage where we all emerge duly influenced by our unique experience. Those who have gone beyond the constraints of the five senses would stand testimony to the preposition that each moment in life is distinct. It is a dynamic combination of a variety of phenomena within and outside a person, both around and beyond one's relative positioning in the environment.

Our understanding of the various facets of life keep changing and refining further as we mature and attain greater profundity. Here are some of the shared versions of the oceanic waves of life experienced by a father and son duo. It is an attempt to unfold the mysteries that are beyond the comprehensions of our simple 'mind', which is the primary driving force in our lives. However, the direction and intrinsic character of the voyage are much beyond the realm of our 'Physical-self'. That is the domain which exists beyond the oscillating 'Cosmic Intelligence', where our pure-self would merge with the 'Spiritual being.'

Having experienced life through the rural landscape as well as the urban, having endured varied levels of scarcity and dealing with the consequent challenges, having danced to the tunes of the human senses with repeated attempts to overcome those base instincts, the gradually surfacing wisdom and normative learnings have flown out as per their level at varying points of time. These generalizations may not hold well across varied spaces or timelines, yet they do generate sparks that could spread more light than heat.

Our life being fluid where things keep changing every moment, the 'Art of Dying' as an incremental learning is important till one takes a stride beyond the cosmic into pure spiritual domain. Marinating under the supervision of a worthy mentor, who enables our perpetual upwardly rise from the lower levels of sustenance to a higher equilibrium, with the growing realisation of being a 'Kabir' within, is sure to arouse the curiosity of a seeker.

The difficult yet plausible vectors that set the direction as well as intrinsic value quotients of the journey are reflected in this book. This is presented through a series of conversations and discussions between the father and the son. If at all these derivatives fail in suggesting the way ahead to many of us, they would at least indicate what is best to avoid. May be with constant sharing of experiences, some of us are able to completely zero down on the ultimate force that invokes the desired thrust.

I tender my humble apologies for any displaced opinion or over emphasizing my limited learnings.

04.12.2021

—Dr. A.P. Maheshwari
NW-118, Soamibagh
Agra-282005
India

Gratitude

I am grateful to my father the late P.S. Maheshwari ji who was my mentor. We often dissented on some of the contents and processes, however, as our ultimate purpose and intent was the same we would pursue the issue till a semblance of an understanding was eventually drawn.

It would be pertinent here to humbly acknowledge the benevolence of two gracious personalities who had a charismatic influence on my Father's spiritual advancement in life- his maternal uncle, most revered Babu Sant Das ji, and later, Babuji's eldest son Shri Nirmal Das ji.

I am also indebted to all those who interacted with him and discussed his views with different perspectives. These free flowing interactions had an energy and creativity of their own & often resulted in innovative interpretations.

I have also gathered the views of various luminaries during my work life while seeking 'wellness domains' for those dealing with the more exacting side of life such as internal security warriors. I am deeply grateful to all my friends, relatives as well as those known and unknown people who have influenced my thought process. And above all my mother who nurtured the best in me through all the ups and downs that life presented.

Any in congruency in depiction is purely due to lack of my understanding or paucity of proper expression on my part. In no way anything be construed otherwise to reflect on the grace of the mentors who remained my role models.

—The author

Contents

1

The Art of Dying

Maybe across different timelines as well as different cultures, the same facts have been explained in their own unique way. Though they may extrinsically appear to be different yet there is a striking resemblance of approach when we scrutinize the journey from the art of living to the art of dying. I had now gradually started observing these twin dimensions as two sides of the same coin.

We generally hear of the 'Art of Living', focussing on some standard tenets of life to seek a seamless confluence of oneself with the surroundings so as to augment the level of visualised or deeply felt inner bliss. I had a chance to undertake a few such courses and as a result evolved into a better adaptation of my earlier self. This was the time when I had joined the Central Reserve Police Force

on deputation and was posted in the conflict-prone areas of lower Assam and later the Kashmir valley. The perpetual violence in these low conflict zones had resulted in the loss of many lives. Such fatalities have different connotations for the Forces and for their adversary. However, on either side, valour continues to be celebrated in its own way with the tag of martyrdom.

One day, during my readings in my free time, I came across the concept of the 'Art of Dying'. This grabbed my attention. It simply stated that we are changing with every moment like a flowing river. The river may appear to be the same but the 'water-flow' keeps changing. Similarly, with each moment several cells cease to exist within us while new cells take birth. With each passing moment, many realisations come to an end and new thoughts capture our mental space. Each moment we die a bit and are also partly reborn within. Our present existence is simply the summation of those moments which we utilise in amplifying our awareness and becoming more inclusive. However, we can't hold on to anything as nothing remains static. Therefore, people who are unable to learn to 'let things go' tend to sink into a state of constant suffering.

This concept made sense as it sounded rather reasonable and appealed to me. I kept mulling over it. In fact, soon enough, I was invited to address a gathering of some people from the local civic society. The audience initially thought that being from the Paramilitary Forces, I would talk of the sacrifices made by our brave hearts in the service of the Nation as they have deeply ingrained feelings of 'Service before self'. But no, I had a different context for them.

The background goes back to my discussions with my father who was a staunch believer of 'Santmat' (Radhasoami), and in particular the first Saint 'Kabir'. Kabir unraveled the truth of the pure, cohesive and everlasting 'Spiritual-self' and denounced the cosmic constituents that sustain on the centrifugal forces. Kabir also focused upon the utmost need for absolute surrender before 'Satguru' (the true spiritual leader), which would include completely relinquishing one's ego and absolving oneself from worldly attachments. We would, accordingly, hold frequent discussions on the intrinsic domains of spirituality. And then he would say, "It is not possible that you hold onto the world and simultaneously attain salvation. You have to 'die' (resurface) and gradually evolve day by day, which means the death of your attachments in this world and simultaneous evolution of the Divine love beyond the domain of death." I found it difficult to accept this interpretation initially, thinking of the 'Art of Living' and would accordingly argue my case with him. I recall him saying, "Yes, indulgence is essential but it should be used tactically. It should not be to boost your desires further but to realise their redundancy in this world and unshackle our 'bondages' here to attain spiritual freedom. That is the real dying or renunciation of the world that would set you free forever. This needs to be firmly embedded in the inner core of our consciousness so that the correct alignments emerge from there." And then he went on to cite three examples from the existing major religions of the world.

"The crucifixion of Christ and then his resurrection after seven days as the 'Son of God' is the core of the Christian belief. The message here is that one has to evolve beyond this world, even at the cost of being crucified.

The second, taking a leaf from the texts of Islam, when Hazrat Ibrahim was asked by Allah to sacrifice what was dearest to him, Hazrat rose to sacrifice his son, who was closest to his heart. Then God, as per the recital, saved his son and accepted his absolute, pure and innocent love towards Him. This was reflected in God's gifting of a pristine white lamb to Ibrahim.

The third, was the belief in Hinduism of Shiva's 'Tandav'. Each person is bound down by the attachments that he nurtures within. It may be anything material or the living. He has to destroy or sacrifice the bondages of all those within him; a 'tandav within' to crossover to the realm of divinity. Don't be misguided by the depiction of 'Tandav' by artists in the form of a storm or destruction of the physical world, as nothing exists on the outside. All that there is, is within us".

Maybe across different timelines as well as different cultures, the same facts have been explained in their own unique way. Though they may extrinsically appear to be different, yet there is a striking resemblance of approach when we scrutinize the journey from the art of living to the art of dying. I had now gradually started observing these twin dimensions as two sides of the same coin.

Following the tenets of Santmat, my dad would eventually conclude, "Detachments alone will prepare you for the take-off stage alone. But to rise above, one needs to internally merge with the holy current with the help of 'Naam'. Recite the holy Name with each breath and surrender yourself to the divine. Practice this consistently as you never know when you would breathe your last." This meditative process became my new 'Art of living'.

My father may not have completely succeeded in the pursuit of what he often preached but I could sense that he constantly wanted to rise upwardly on this path of complete submission to his Guru and kept trying to achieve that state just like 'Eklavya'.

Our life goes through a constant process of change and evolution. Life, the constant tutor, has taught us that there is no finality in this dynamic world and that it has its own balancing act, which will always remain a mystery for us. Yet we can sail through life satisfactorily if we get some meaningful insight into the art of living as well as the art of dying. Having redefined the art of living, I could grasp the relevance of the 'Art of Dying' with greater clarity as the art of letting go, forgiving and forgetting. Our desires and attachments need to gradually die every day. We need neither be a slave of our body nor the mind. We need to crossover these thresholds in order to become free from bondage within the realm of our consciousness.

Even our desperation to hold on to a dying person only adds to his sufferings. And one day we were also put to this test when my father fell terminally ill and had to undergo surgery. It was 4:30 in the afternoon when I got a frantic message from the hospital to reach the ICU immediately. The doctor declared, "We can keep him alive for a few days on the machine but only in a state of coma or you let him go now." We decided to let him go and he departed for his heavenly abode peacefully.

Those who were close to him knew that he was

mentally prepared to leave this world. Post death, the serene smile on his face was a sublime indicator of his absolute sense of contentment and readiness to quit his earthly form. My father's constant effort eventually, through a process of elimination, had slowly but surely resulted in his mastering the art of dying. By absolute submission to his Guru succeeded in setting himself free from the bondages within him. He often said, "Devote your energy to try and assimilate the dispersed divine element back from your physical self and carry it to the seat of your conscience for an upward thrust. The transition would then be smooth. A spiritually inclined death is the ultimate gateway to the divine domain. Such a departure is the only positive forward leap to liberate yourself from all the bondages and vicissitudes of pain, pleasure and grief."

At this stage, I am reminded of one of the tales of a sufi singer, who was invited to sing in the court of an emperor. He was popular for his collection of songs and melodious voice with which he sang each couplet, totally lost in the divine. When he was asked by the emperor, 'Why are you describing everything in such a non-affirmative way?' He responded, "It is not by choice but that I find myself incapable of expressing it any other way". The emperor was furious, 'You are unsure about God? .... He is not air.

He is not water. He is not sun. You have the audacity to insult the Almighty. This is no way of singing the praise of God!' The singer humbly responded, 'We can know what 'He' actually is only after rising above the illusions of this world.'

As a corollary to this understanding, my father also focused upon the concept of 'Die empty'. Emptiness is the only state of fullness in this ephemeral world. We have to free ourselves of our base instincts, needs and attachments in order to graduate to the higher level. Hence, 'Die empty' is the necessary condition for each level in our upwardly mobile journey. Every level has its own bondages. Hence, they need to be nullified 'in toto' in order to rise to the next level. This can also be understood in terms of mitigating one's Karmic burdens at each level within the cosmic domains.

'Kabir' has conveyed the absolute truth in this context as follows :

Sai seti na paiye, Baatan mile na koye,
Kabir sauda 'Naam' ka, Sir bin Kabhun na hoye !!

Thou shall not beget the divine without earning it, nor shall you attain 'Him' by mere discourse. To successfully connect with the ultimate, the 'Naam', one needs to mature, totally immerse oneself in order to marinate and make the ultimate sacrifice; and that would be akin to laying your head on a chopping board. It implies that one needs to be in a state of absolute surrender and conjoin with the inner chord of sound that emanates from the epicenter of the 'Ultimate Consciousness'. This can only happen when we internalize with every single breath that we take. Extrinsic utterances are of no use. Oblation of one's 'Head' also implies completely neutralizing the mind and crushing the 'ego'. This is the intrinsic process of 'Die empty' at each level. Kabir, in one of his *Shabads,* **'Sadho ee murdan ka gaon'** has further highlighted the redundancy of anything and everything in the cosmic domain.

We may accept these narrations or we may not, but nonetheless experimental learnings do underscore the art of dying and the forward leap beyond.......!

□

2

Draupadi Episode: Unravelling another Layer

Eventually, the senses having played with the soul in their own egoistic or insane adherence to their inbuilt tendency, carry the soul to that point of desperation where it now feels deceived, fully corrupted and sold out. In that state of destitution and abandonment, the soul, if it has managed to preserve its spiritual chastity, reverts to its inner core with a genuine yearning for the 'Supreme Being'.

The Mahabharata has been read and interpreted in so many ways, relating different interesting episodes with the dynamics of our life. It also leads us to the spiritual domains of the ultimate 'Truth'. Different people interpret the 'Truth' differently as per their level of spiritual evolution and assessment capabilities.

"I am not trying to find any backward or forward linkages to the perspective that I am going to reproduce, but rather to focus on the intrinsic concept that it eventually zeros down to", so asserted my father.

As we know, the conduct of the Pandavas has often been under scrutiny despite their having some unique individual qualities that placed them on a higher pedestal in comparison to a mere commoner. Losing their kingdom, losing themselves and then their own wife in a game of dice overshadows the very best of their virtues, skills and exceptional wisdom. Not delving deep in the maze of controversies that surround the Draupadi episode, attention is drawn to crucial happenings due to highly questionable conduct of the Kauravas which ranged from a lack of decorous behavior to the aspersions of treating a woman as a mere commodity.

One of the spiritual interpretations of this defining episode that flowed from some quarters seem to be intriguing, particularly while attempting to understand life in its peculiar formats.

Draupadi was married to the five 'Pandava' brothers. During the various trials and tribulations that the Pandavas had to face in their lives, there came a point where they found themselves so helpless that they were left with no choice but to put Draupadi at stake as a 'bet' in a game of dice against the 'Kauravs'. And when in the most demeaning display of depravity and callousness, the Kauravs attempt to disrobe her in full public view in court, then in desperation the aggrieved, mocked, disgraced lady, left to fend for herself, heartbroken lady pleads for the protection of her honour to Lord Krishna. It is then that God comes to her rescue and what follows is common knowledge. As the Kauravs begin to tug at her saree, it keeps on unravelling, fold after fold with no end in sight leaving the Kaurav brothers perplexed, frustrated and eventually exhausted.

The relevant segment of the whole saga is reproduced in the margins to ease its understanding:

Draupadi's Cheer-Haran, literally meaning stripping of one's clothes, marks a definitive moment in the story of the Mahabharata. It is the central reason of the Mahabharata war, intensifying the rivalry between Pandavas and Kauravas to a point of no return where nothing less than the others' demise could satiate their hatred and assuage the crushed pride of the Pandvas.

Yudhishthira and his four brothers were the rulers of Indraprastha under the sovereignty of Emperor Dhritarashtra. Dhritarashtra's son Duryodhana, who resided in the capital of the empire Hastinapur, was always jealous of his cousins. Together with his brothers, his friend Karna and maternal uncle Shakuni, he conspired to call the Pandavas at Hastinapur and win their kingdoms in a game of dice called chauser. Shakuni was an inveterate gambler and very skilled at winning by unfair means. The idea was that Shakuni will play against Yudhishthira and win at the gambling table what was impossible to win at the battlefield.

As the game progressed, Yudhishthira lost all his wealth and kingdom one by one. Having lost all material wealth, he went on to put his brothers at stake one by one and lost them too. Ultimately, he put himself at stake, and lost again. All the Pandavas were now the slaves of Kauravas. But for the villain Shakuni, the humiliation of the Pandavas was not complete. He plods Yudhishthira that he has not lost everything yet. Yudhishthira still has Draupadi with him and if he wishes he can win everything back by putting Draupadi at stake. Yudhishthira walks into the trap and to the horror of everybody present, puts Draupadi as a bet for the next round. Shakuni rolls the dice and gleefully shouts "Look, I have won." Duryodhana commands his younger brother Dushasana to forcefully bring Draupadi into the forum. Dushasana barges into the living quarters of Draupadi who had just finished her bath and was drying her loose hair. Dushasan grabs her by the hair and brings her into the court dragging her by the hair.

Unable to withstand the distress of his wife, an emotional Bhima even threatens to burn up Yudhishthira's hands with which he placed Draupadi on stake. Arjun tries to help Draupadi but Yudhisthira forbids him. Bhima vows to cut off Dushasana's hands. Arjun vows to kill Karna for insulting his wife.

Now in an emotional appeal to the elders present in the forum, Draupadi repeatedly questions the legitamacy of Yudhishthira's right to place her at stake, when he himself had lost his freedom and as a consequence did not possess any property in the first place. Everybody remains dumbfounded. Bhishma, the patriarch of the Kaurava family and a formidable warrior, has only this explanation to offer to Draupadi: "The course of morality is subtle and even the illustrious wise in this world fail to always understand it." He now commands the Pandavas to strip themselves in the manner of slaves. They obey by stripping off their upper garments.

Then Kauravas demand the same from Draupadi, who is inconsolable. Then to the horror of everybody present, Dushasana proceeds to strip off Draupadi's sari. Seeing her husbands unable or unwilling to help her, Draupadi prays to Lord Krishna to protect her modesty. Lord Krishna now works a miracle so that as Dushasana unwraps layers and layers of her sari, her sari keeps getting extended. Seeing Draupadi being violated so brazenly, Bhima in a roaring rage, vows to tear open Dushasana's breast one day and drink his blood. Finally, a tired Dushasana backs off without being able to strip Draupadi.

Draupadi is the exemplification of bhakti to God. She showed utmost faith in Lord Krishna.

All of us are aware that story-telling has been a strong medium of communication. Various episodes are often interwoven to complete a picture that may otherwise appear like the elephant from the Panchatantra tale that was described by five blind people in five different ways as per their own interpretation of the animal. However, what matters is not the description or the semantics of expressions but the hidden message it emanates to help us understand and make our lives better.

"Stop diverting your attention elsewhere and listen to me carefully", father would candidly tell all those present particularly when he was discussing a crucial issue. "Our five senses are like the Pandavas to whom Draupadi, the soul, has been wedded to. Without knowing the intricacies of each sensual enslavement, the soul keeps playing to the tune of each of our five senses blindly, willingly and sometimes even helplessly under some given delusion. Eventually, the senses having played with the soul in their own insane adherence to their intrinsic tendency, carry the soul to that point of desperation where it now feels cheapened, deceived, corrupted and sold out. In that state of destitution and abandonment, the soul, if it has managed to preserve its spiritual chastity, reverts to its inner core in a genuine yearning before the 'Supreme Being'. It is this realisation of the redundancy of the senses and the eternal relevance of the Godly element, along with a final merger with the ultimate 'Truth', that the soul is embraced by the 'Beloved'. This is akin to the 'Crucifixion' in this world by one's own people or the 'dance of destruction' amidst bondages within or the sacrificing of the external attachments. Once liberated from the clutches of the senses and its indulgences, there is nothing that holds you back from a natural merger with the divine consciousness."

The above interpretation, though often cited by my father, initially failed to hold much appeal to us. However, gradually with time it emerged as being increasingly pertinent with a deeper understanding of the relevance of spirituality that we experienced in life with its various 'ups & downs'. I am incapable of interpreting it further as I find myself wanting. However, I am humbly sharing the concept just in case it helps you in your life to navigate better, as it did to me with the gradual emergence of a deeper awareness. Before I conclude this thought, I would like to draw your attention to certain concepts that it draws our focus upon. Three important aspects that flow from this episode are:

-Realizing the redundancy and manipulative characteristics of our senses beyond a point during our passage through worldly indulgences;

-True yearning for the divine with a sense of absolute surrender from within and

-Letting the divinity flow unhindered, where oneself becomes neither the body nor the mind.

However, these things are experiential and beyond logic. Hence, I concede accordingly.

□

3

Take a Balcony view of Self

The concept of a 'balcony view' has helped most of us reposition ourselves better on the grid of this dynamic life. This creates a more conducive environment of mutual sustenance based on shared vision. It promotes a self-corrective, non-conflicting approach to handle untoward happenings. The opportunity cost and its optimisation is the key when viewed holistically.

If someone were to ask me: "What is life all about?" I would, after so many years of oscillating experiences, say: "Life is basically a process of attempting to repeatedly enhance our level of awareness." On the face of it, it may sound too simplistic and obvious. But those who have completed the vicious circle of fending off adversities in life may like to recall that– "The more things change, the more they remain the same," which is followed by the dictum: "Whatever has to happen, shall happen."

My father would often reiterate that the Saints have persistently laid emphasis on one significant aspect of life, that, it is a self-propelled continuous flow of consciousness that becomes distorted and displaced by the volatility of the mind which is governed by a play of the senses and one's run away ego. Accordingly, everyone has a perception of 'oneself' as well as of the 'others'. Here there are strong probabilities that it could be severely infested with a motley of biases. How do we come out of this self-created entanglement? Similarly, over a period of time, we develop our own learnings and interpretation patterns, better understood as stereotyping, which leads to a fixity of cognitions. How do we neutralise the effect of these filters?

Generally, a policeman questions the character of a person till proven otherwise. Similarly, the perception about a cop would be negative unless he proves to be otherwise. Such incongruencies in our life distort the reality. In fact, nearly eighty per cent of the time we live a life based on these predisposed perceptions. The 'reality-assessment' often remains a myth.

The profession of a policeman is similar to those other professions that come into play during various

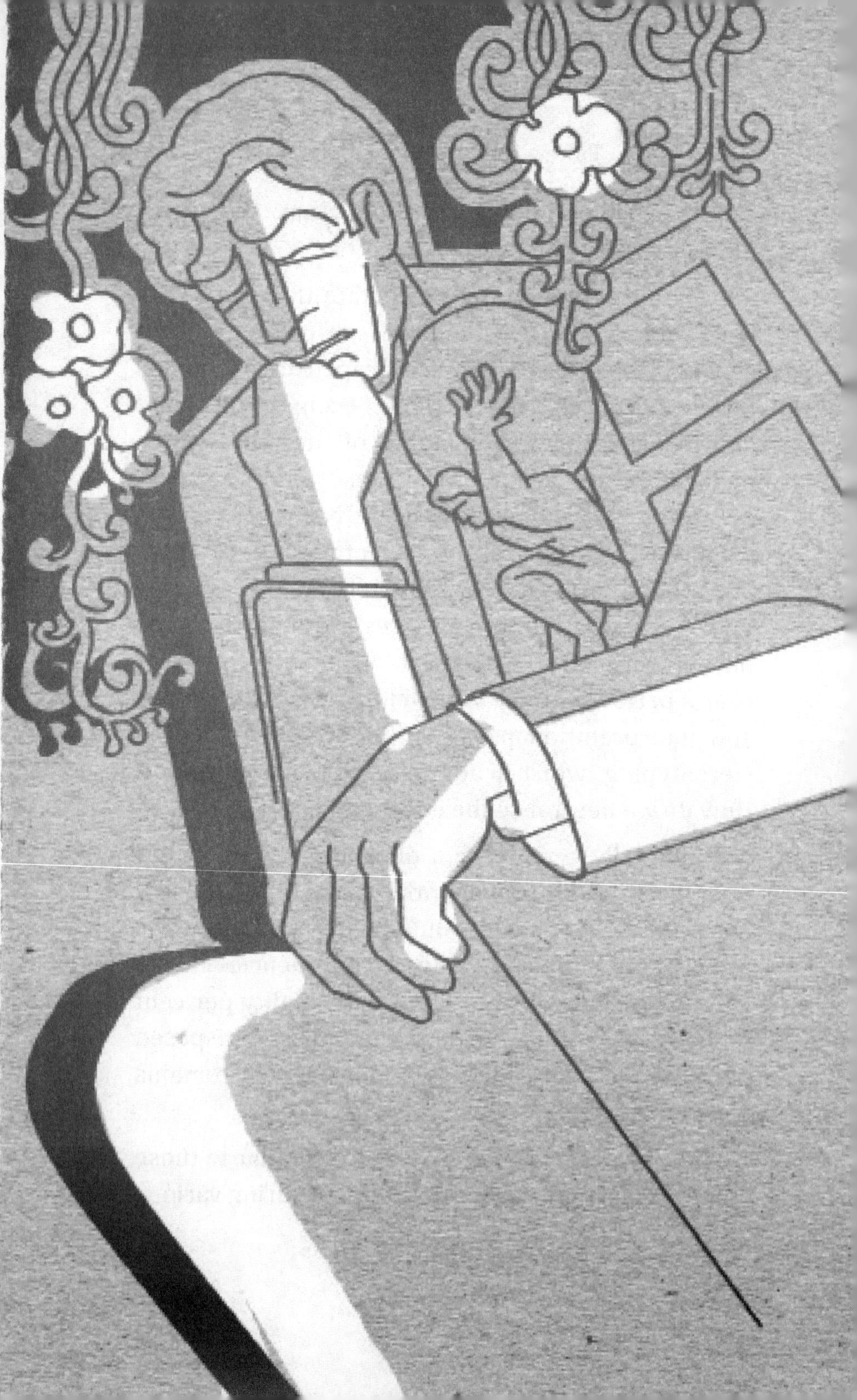

emergency situations. A policeman encounters a multitude of haranguing and unfathomable situations where diverse conflicts keep emerging. At times, it becomes difficult to unearth the underlying layers of hidden reality. Such situations are eventually managed on the oscillating continuum of power brokers or at best the art of proportionate balancing.

What is true about the individual is true about the community too. Hence, often one finds that the evolved folks in life insist on periodically taking a balcony view of issues on hand. The area of operation could be anywhere; school, family circles or society at large. However, I was lucky to have understood to some degree this concept through the narrations of my father who had imbibed them from his maternal uncle. His maternal uncle himself was an enlightened soul. At his level, divinity or the truth were more experiential than by observation.

So, what does it mean to us? Those who have gone into the depth of our behavioral patterns have invariably insisted upon the periodical course corrections with neutralisation of the mind as it has an inherent tendency to develop some biases. When left free, it tends to play into the cradle of the human senses and generates responses that are not fully congruent with the rules of stability and positive sustenance. The deep mind, under its intelligence domain, generates an auto response mechanism based on a distorted set of inputs. When a due sense of proportion and proper discretion are not adhered to, such dichotomies creep in. So the experienced souls caution us repeatedly to pluck away the evil growth at its initial stage. Else, later on in life they would become deep rooted and we will find ourselves unable to uproot them.

Hence, it is deemed imperative to take a posture where we can observe ourselves dispassionately as an observer and audit each action objectively. This calls for careful introspection and taking corrective action to tame the 'wild elephant' within.

Before we go ahead, let us dwell on a story focusing on behavioural responses. A child was sitting on the edge of a well and likely to slip and fall. His mother tried her level best to cajole him into realizing this and coming back. But the child refused to budge. Frantic, the lady went running to a nearby spiritual practitioner and sought his help. The saint advised, "Why don't you take another child along to sit on an adjoining wall further away from the well and beckon your son to join him. You will see that the congener will have a greater influence." And that's exactly how it played out. The first child soon joined the second one. Peer pressure matters. The question now is that who is the best congener? Unless one gets a mentor who has succeeded in attaining the ultimate truth, our conscience then remains our best congener. Hence, a balcony approach calls for the right alignment within us as well.

We have to understand both the physics and chemistry of our physiology well, in order to be in a better position to initiate neutralisation procedures. These could range from physical yoga, games, music to just being blissfully alone and meditative. The need here is to be open, inclusive and non-intrusive. Accept the situation and accordingly become more and more aware and responsible. That would then lead us to take upon ourselves the responsibility of whatever is happening in our life. And thus we would keep our focus on fixing the issue rather than falling in conflict with somebody or wasting time otherwise. Having done that, it becomes easy to do an impartial self-audit under an enlightened thought process and retract on the desired path.

Even when one deals with individuals, or groups such as families, communities, organisations, societies or nations, one needs to evolve a process of a self-audit that would be relevant for the environment in which they sustain. Simultaneously we need to consider the mechanism that provides the engines or drivers for growth for these groups. It is there that we recognise the co-existence of each stakeholder and go on to create a win-win situation for all. We would ultimately realise not only the need but also the urgency of the correctness of means. We shall then witness its multiplier effect on our internal strength–the safety quotient against destabilising forces.

The concept of a 'balcony view' has helped most of us to reposition ourselves better on the grid of this dynamic life. This creates a more conducive environment of mutual sustenance based on shared vision. It promotes a self-corrective, non-conflicting approach to handle untoward happenings. The opportunity cost and its optimisation is the key when viewed holistically. When we take a balcony view, we become substantially holistic as well as assimilative in our approach.

When the sages adopted a balcony view they realised how lust, anger, greed and similar negative forces tend to make the mind volatile. On the other hand how contentment, forgiveness, kindness and such positive vectors could help align the mind to the holistic center of gravity.

To understand this truth, it will not be out of place to revisit the *Kabir Baani*:

Kaam, Krodh, Mad, Lobh bisaro,
Yehi baat asal ki;
Sheel, Kshama, Daya chit dharo,
Kahat Kabira dil ki.

Kabir pours out his heart to assert that the real self should be full of patience, forgiveness, kindness and shun greed, lust, anger and intoxication in order to tread the right path. This is part of his *Shabad* where he does a reality check with the advice that with every breath one should only try to do good deeds and attempt to connect with the holy sound (*Naam*) within. Life is so unpredictable that whilst you may be blissfully active one minute the other you may breathe your last. And then you are no better than the gravel that lies under the dense foliage of the forest.

One may find this concept vague, but exponentially it has helped me to elevate my consciousness and have a holistic view of life. Only those who practice it can absorb this better. My apologies to those who find my assertion ambiguous.

□

4

3D Approach to Life

I have thus grown up with the understanding that not only thoughts but also our conduct as well as the response to any situation should be guided by the principles of divinity, which are the principles of our creation. In the emotional sense that would mean being humble, patient, kind and helpful to all. We must try to add euphoria to the life of people and if we cannot do that then at best stay neutral rather than generating an adverse impact.

Life comes with many ups and downs. In fact, experience teaches that if on a particular day you are not facing challenges, then it is an indicator that you may not be on the right path. Life is dynamic and always demands a congruent response. Any task or activity remains difficult or formidable in life only to the extent where there is a response capacity deficit.

Hence, the real risk in life is not the situation per se, but the paucity of appropriate tools, tactics and commitment. These determine the risk quotient. Driving on a highway was a risk only till I did not have enough expertise and exposure. Swimming was a threat until I had trained myself well. My father had his own way of looking at things. His strategy for problem-solving had three distinct components that he would usually apply. He had a deep understanding of the human sustenance as a sub-system within a much larger, in fact unbounded, 'super system' that runs on 'auto-mode'. He propounded it as a 3D approach. The first 'D' is *Dawa* (the medicine, the technique to win over the incongruities). When a doctor examines us, he first conducts a diagnosis of the problem by going into the history, undertakes analysis of the existing parameters and goes ahead with the validation tests as per his assessment. Similarly, any problem-solution initially entails due diagnostic exercise, which results in providing various options for remedies that are potent, feasible and affordable. It essentially takes us to the cost benefit matrix. However, an experienced practitioner will also carefully analyse in detail the response capacity of the system that may require lifestyle changes, so that an adequate absorption and saturation process follows. These aspects are being highlighted only to stress the need to understand the

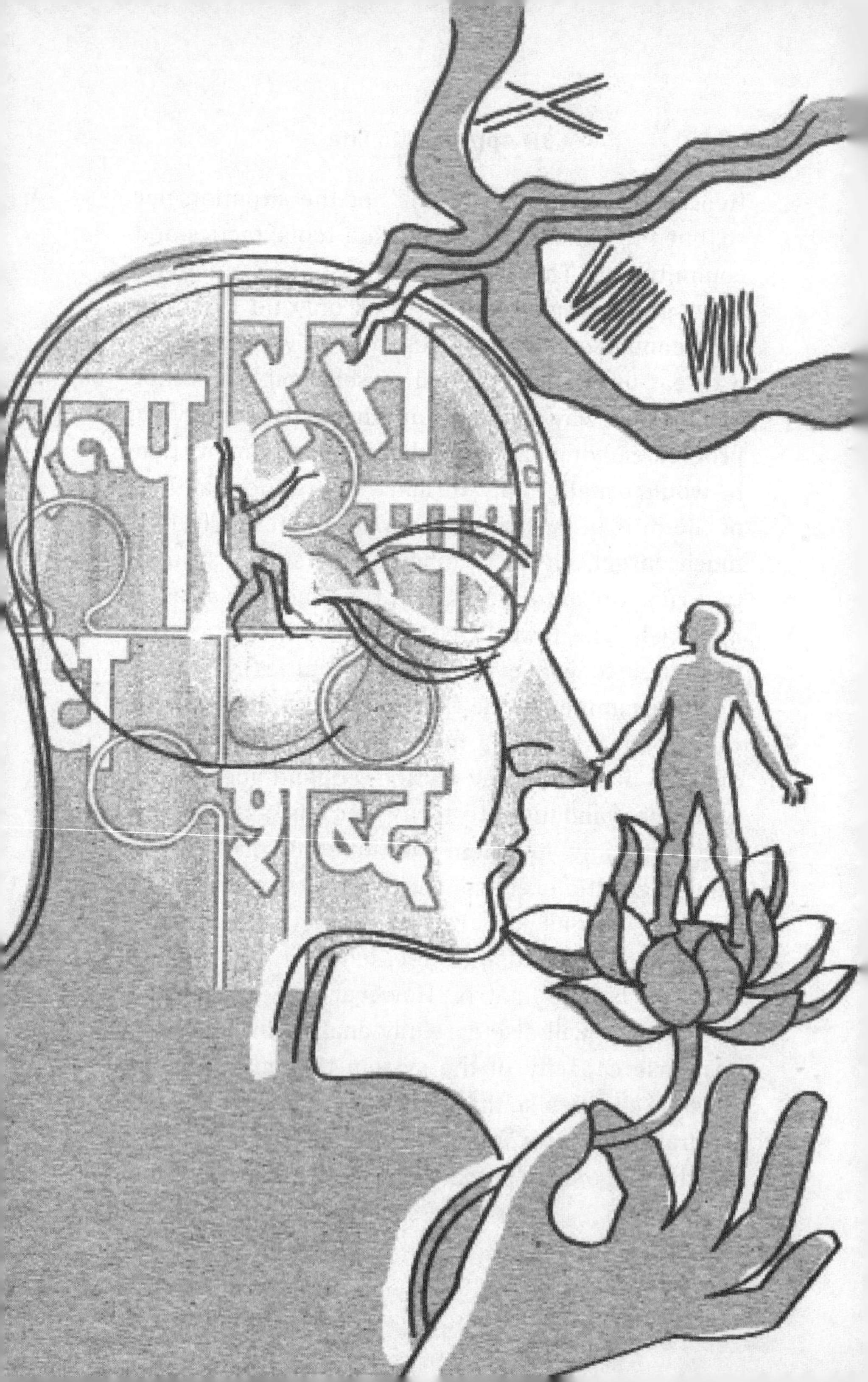

perspectives when we zero down upon the *Dawa*, an appropriate problem-solution option.

As I mentioned above, my father always believed that we are part of a much larger, endless creation. All entities in the Creation are mutually connected through the reflections and impressions of their thoughts, intentions as well as actions. The level of divinity or the segment of the divine element as nurtured by a person 'within', sets the level of his positioning on the grid of this perpetual creation. Initially I did not believe it. But with growing awareness and continual process of inner 'marination', I too started experiencing what he advised. Since, this aspect can only be individually experienced, logic is seldom enough to absorb or imbibe this truth.

The second aspect led him to focus on the other 'D' called *Dua* (the good wishes or prayers flowing from other beings around in one's favour). Divinity is present in all forms of existence. And this we need to remember in order to define the context at any point of time. Hence, goodness, kindness, helping the destitute, compassion and empathy manifested by cogent responses in these domains at the individual level generate the circles of *Dua* for us. These positive waves entering our life strengthen our resolve and mitigate negativity. This is purely based on the law of attraction in its widest possible connotation. Thus, a blissful existence will come with an inseparable bonding of *Dua*. Happiness may be connected with an outwardly source, but bliss is sourced from within and is seamless. The merger with the divine element starts with such selfless sharing coupled with self-denial and a state of detachment. This means that you can't blissfully part with any of your deemed belongings unless you first detach yourself from it. Then we can open endless vistas of the higher energy levels which further empowers us and the problem becomes miniscule. As we raise our level, the law of attraction also comes into play. I would take a detour here to briefly discuss the intrinsics of the 'Secret'.

Our sages and ancestors had actually simplified the process to a great extent. We probably could not comprehend the depth of their simple expressions that could change the entire purpose of our life. Although we became more and more literate and knowledgeable in the worldly sense but our intrinsic understanding of the core concepts remained shallow as our life shifted from experiential facets in grounded reality to laboratory based validations. "And this is beyond any science", my father would often announce. He had experientially learnt that our thoughts decided our course of life. All his actions and reactions were monitored with his 'deity' in the forefront. I have thus grown up with the understanding that not only thoughts but also our conduct as well as the response to any situation should be guided by the principles of divinity, which are far more superior to the principles of our cosmic creation. In the emotional sense that would mean being humble, patient, kind and helpful to all. We must try to add euphoria to the life of people and if we cannot do that then at best stay neutral rather than generating an adverse impact.

"Although I have total faith in *Mauj* (the natural flow of divinity), my mind at times 'deviates' and wavers," my father would repeatedly confess. But then he would again and again push himself to visualising the spectrum of positivity placing the Supreme-being (our benefactor) above all. Harmonisation with the natural flow of creation sends signals to the universe to rearrange your surroundings in accordance with your visualisation. One then tends to merge with the *Mauj* of the Master and quietly assumes command of his own life. Starting from Kabir to Nanak, the entire galaxy of our saints have in their own way spoken of the alignment with the supreme creator and his creation.

The ultimate experience is that of *Daya* (the showering of divine grace & mercy). When we surrender our self to the inner self beyond the limitation of our mind and ego, divinity then flows in brimming our energy levels. Yoga is not merely a physical exercise. In fact, it goes far beyond that. It is actually the absolute alignment of our body, mind and emotion with our pure-self (*Surat*). When we shed our ego, when our mind is wholly neutralised, it is then that we become all inclusive and self-responsive. The level and inert sense of awareness goes on to become endless. We accept in totality whatever is happening around us and stand in complete gratitude without an iota of grievance or resentment. In this context, I also quote below the four crisp principles of prayer before the Divine:

- Genuine repentance for not being in complete alignment with the Creator.
- Genuine yearning to be forgiven, an admission of guilt backed by the will to re-emerge.
- Absolute surrender to the Creator and acceptance of all that is happening around us, governed by the forces of creation.
- Eternal gratitude for being accepted inspite of all our human failings.

The realisation that we are lacking in absolute response and the very admission of this incompetence is the initial step forward. With this realisation, we discover humility and can move further by pleading for forgiveness of the Divine. Then follows complete surrender and absorption; which is the state of an ultimate expression of love. We then surrender ourselves to 'His' benign grace and mercy. Despite our shortcomings, when this element of God engulfs us, then a deep sense of gratitude pervades our being.

In order to lay more emphasis my father would explain further: "It is easy to say *Daya*, but it is difficult to realise it. It comes only with complete acceptance and a complete assimilation of the self with boundless gratitude, which is the state of absolute surrender and devotion. There is no place for religiosity. It is complete spirituality. The deity is not important. The values, which the deity radiates or reflects, absorption of those values is the crux. By merely hero worshipping the teacher we won't imbibe the lessons. When we actually practice what he teaches, is when we elevate ourselves from within. Hence, *Daya* is coupled with total adherence to those values, their absorption as well as their saturation within us. Akin to the complete hollowness of a flute, symbiotically by dispensing with our ego and the superficial mind, we will open the flood gates of the divine energy that is constantly overlapping our surroundings. Like all the other energy wave lengths that we have discovered in this world today with its matching frequency receptors, we also need to tune our personal machine called our body to invite the flow of the divine energies. Following certain practices we can delve deep within and connect with the divine. The soul and the Divine must have unhindered connect. To put it simply, the *Santmat* practices focus on '*Surat-shabd*' meditation. Internalised focus is supported by the sound and light manifestations that are the transmitting factors of 'energy' at different gradients. These are the essential tools needed to seek *Daya* within, where 'Shabd' undoutedly remains the prime vector."

The 3D tools, *Dawa*, *Dua* and *Daya* thus retain distinct importance in treading the dynamism of life! A huge demonstration effect then sets in. It is time to grasp the basics of life again amidst its dynamic facets. I was fortunate enough to remain closely associated with a few such people who followed these principles and they became my direct or indirect mentors.

□

5

Be a Kabir Within

Being 'Kabir' would mean detaching from all the things that take your attention away from the ultimate goal. It would also mean adopting the right virtues that become strong drivers for the upward thrust. Understanding the cause and effect relationship and accordingly enhancing your level of awareness is another crucial aspect. For managing anything, unless we give our hundred per cent, it is not possible to get the synergy needed to break the inertia and get into the mode of criticality.

"If we take a system's approach to life, then we are all a part of a larger system." Over time, the environmental context of our holistic sustenance has been explained in multi-contextual formats. The externalities are defined in terms of a scientific configuration to its geographical relevance and the socio-cultural and economic domains along with

"Karat-Karat Abhyas ke Jadmati hot Sujaan

their impact on human relationships. Within these realms, we understand ourselves as the physical self, emotional self, logical self and the social self. The multiplicity of interactive transactions has been carefully observed, assessed and then elaborated in the form of various management practices and value codes that are pertinent for a given situation. We all have gone through varied expositions and experimental facets and have tried to redefine the vectors that may lead to our 'perceived' state of success. It is difficult to decipher 'Kabir' by our logical self or our mind alone, as he says that he has himself experienced the 'truth', while we have been disseminating it as an observer through our secondary bookish knowledge.

We follow of 'Kabir', who is regarded as the first *Saint* (the sage who amalgamated with the ultimate). We draw our personal and social code of conduct from his verses. At the cost of repetition, spiritually, for us it is meant that we should control our senses, thus, emancipating our soul from their slavery. It also implies neutralising any form of obsession with them. It further means adopting upward drivers in the form of good virtues ranging from forgiveness, complete surrender before the Creator and being in an absolute state of gratitude. Once this take-off state is achieved, the Soul (*Surat*) then has to be connected through sound (*Shabd or Naam as prime vector*) and corresponding light energies via '*Surat-Shabd*' practices with the flow of the pure current that constantly emanates within us, from the original abode of Consciousness. In other words, there is nothing outside, all that there is, is within. The only way 'OUT' (from all the problems, deceptions or illusions) is 'IN' (within our purest-self, the Supreme element *Surat*).

The outside environment is volatile and dynamic. One person crosses over to the inside blissfully while the other one undergoes incessant grief. This compels us to put a few questions to ourselves. We generally judge any phenomena through our mental logic that may actually only be half the truth, being limited by our individual vision. Accordingly, neutrality of the mind and enhancement of our awareness without any predisposed mental block is the fundamental condition for our ascent towards the final truth. Kabir experienced it himself. Hence, he was certain that there is only one version.

Once the realisation dawns upon us it is then that we start accepting what is happening around us. We then start holding only ourselves responsible for it and now assume the charge of elevating ourselves beyond that given wretched situation. Even those who have been most successful in managing their life, focus upon an inclusive and assimilative sustenance for synergetic outcomes. Kabir focuses on the internalised elevation. If we manage our 'own self' well, rest will automatically fall in place.

Kabir says, "Only the one who is ready to set his house ablaze, can traverse with me." The house here embodies the entanglements within which our inner self is caged:

Jo ghar phoonke aapna,
Chale hamare saath!

Here I would also like to narrate an interesting ancient tale. A parrot was caged for its beauty and melodious voice by a bird catcher. He sold it to a merchant who hailed from a distant land. The parrot now began to strongly yearn for his natural surroundings. After a few years when the merchant was once again revisiting the land of the parrot, he asked the parrot if it wanted anything from its homeland. The parrot replied, 'Kindly tell my near and dear ones about my whereabouts and enquire about their wellbeing.' The merchant, during his visit, met the family and friends of that parrot and gave its message. Suddenly, one of the relatives of the parrot collapsed. The merchant repented having spoken to the parrot's family. On his return, the parrot back-home asked him about his relatives. The merchant narrated the whole episode including the collapsing of the relative of the parrot. As soon as the parrot heard the story, he too collapsed. The poor merchant cursed himself for having told the truth as now he had lost his parrot as well. He opened the cage door and threw the parrot out of the cage. The next moment the parrot flew off flapping its wings and perched itself on a nearby tree. The baffled merchant asked the parrot why it had done this to him. The parrot replied, 'My congener has taught me this trick using you as the medium'. Taking a cue from this tale, the saints assert that man is caged in this world through his own senses. One needs to be dead in order to escape this worldly cage, which is akin to destroying ones worldly abode or attachments.

The will and inclination to detach, sacrifice, deny oneself is the starting point of the journey. These very bondages contribute to our release and our upwardly incline along with a stabilising effect.

Bandhan se bandhan katen,
Nirbandh hojaye!

According to Kabir, our body is merely a bare piece of cloth, wrapped around our core self, the soul. Man enslaved by his never ending lust and avarice vitiates the purity of this cover. The balance between the decadent forces such as greed, lust, jealousy and ego against the virtuous mobile vectors like humility, kindness, compassion, forgiveness and gratitude often remain heavily displaced. However, an enlightened soul keeps the purity intact even after traversing through myriad oscillations during this life.

Jhini jhini beeni chadariya ...
Jyon ki tyon dhar deeni chadariya!

And when it comes to practicality, the art of attaining this level, Kabir made it appear very simple–You just need to numb your three major senses–the eyes, ears and mouth from the externalities and focus on the inner self. Its assimilation with the humming sound resonating within us would pull us to the higher levels of its origin. Such a meditative process shall levitate us to connect with the 'Super-Self'. He has unfolded the experiential truth much beyond the comprehension of our mind-driven 'logical-self' where the conclusions are always based on superficial truths at any given point of time. These superficial truths are based on secondary data and observations, which are likely to have illusionary interpretations. But truth is one and only one.

Aankh, kaan, Munh band Karao,
Anhad jhinga shabad sunao!

In the whole process, Kabir has repeatedly laid stress on the indispensability of the *Guru*, a mentor for guiding our path. The mentor who has to be valued for what he teaches and not for his physical self. Kabir prohibits rituals. Rituals lead to *status quo* and are, therefore, forbidden in our spiritual journey. Once we advance from one level to the next, we may need a more seasoned mentor. If we get a mentor, who has attained the ultimate in divinity that would obviously be ideal. Else we need to rise level by level under the supervision of the right mentors at each level. Hence, dynamism is a reality in those zones too. Since the mind is all powerful and is capable of creating fallacies, an enlightened mentor shall help us sail through with ease. An inexperienced mentor may give us wrong directions and therefore, even if we work hard with utmost dedication, it would be futile.

Guru kiya hai deh ka,
Satguru chinha nahi;
Bhausagar ke jaal main,
Phir phir gota khain!

And the ultimate wisdom that Kabir partakes is that real majestic power shall be blissfully enjoyed only by the one who has no outwardly desire—no deviations.

Jisko kachhu na chahiye,
Wohi shahanshah!

The entire self-management philosophy hovers around an awareness of our own 'machine'- the way it is configured, the inherent tendencies or features of each component as well as their holistic functioning. How best we deal with it, given the dynamics of life, remains a constant challenge for all those who are keen to levitate from within.

To sum it up, being a Kabir 'within' would mean choosing a right, honest goal; adopting an erudite and compelling mentor who really knows the path one needs to pursue and has himself gained prior experience in traversing across smoothly to get to the designated goal. Being 'Kabir' would mean detaching from all the things that take your attention away from the ultimate goal. It would also mean adopting the right virtues that become strong drivers for the upward thrust. Understanding the cause and effect relationship and accordingly enhancing your level of awareness is another crucial aspect. For managing anything, unless we give our hundred per cent, it is not possible to garner the synergy needed to break the inertia and get into a mode of criticality. Identifying the epicentre of the 'ultimate-destination' and internalising with the innermost chord that will pull us towards it holds the key. The whole Creation would then realign itself to facilitate our journey.

Thus, there are different ways of understanding Kabir. But the best is to look 'within' and immerse ourselves completely there.

□

6

Determine Your Level

Our level shifts from laying stress on the physical as well as cosmic self to the spiritual self and from self-aggrandising to absolute humility, moulding our synergetic responses accordingly. At this stage, we align with the upwardly directed vectors without falling in conflict with our surroundings.

Years back, as a child, I overheard my father discussing with my elder sister about the core concept that determines one's level (*Ghat*). He spoke to her about constantly striving to ascend from one ghat to the next in order to shed the subordinate level bondages and access higher level equilibriums. Then I could not completely comprehend what he was trying to get at. He went on to further elaborate, to "Lali", as was his endearing term when addressing my elder sister, "If you are sitting on the ground, then that will have its own drawbacks. There may be creepy crawlies troubling you here, so you would rise and seat yourself on a chair." Similarly, in your mental and spiritual space when you exist at a particular level, despite some advantages which are also bound to be there, the negative flows of that state would also begin to impact, vitiate or obstruct. Hence, again the answer is that one now needs to elevate further. On this issue of determining one's level father had a tale to narrate. It goes like this–a cobbler happened to go to a perfume market one day and fell unconscious. People called several doctors but they failed to bring him back to his senses. Suddenly, a passerby recognised him and said, "Give me a moment. I know him well. He is a cobbler from our area." He then took off his shoe and put it next to the cobbler's nose. The smell of the leather, immediately revived him, bringing him back to his senses. This amusing tale dwells on the intrinsic level of a person and his potential in its own way.

Most of us understand Maslow's theory within behavioural domains, which propounds five different levels of hierarchies that are more relevant to the human inner-motivational grid. Starting with the lowest level, which is money and material resources, then next in hierarchy comes security in life; followed by love and affection which become driving motivators; then comes prestige, fame or the need to

be recognised and finally at the apex comes the stage of self-actualisation–the unending zeal for creativity and overcoming challenges. This could be a good way of managing the folks in a work space by raising their motivational level, thus converting them and thereby empowering them as high achievers in life. However, the experience over a period of time partially negated the premise that these different states or levels are strictly hierarchical in nature. In fact, they appear to follow a random pattern that does not appear to be completely logical and may even be irrational and erratic. This is true about the cosmic domains. Nonetheless, once we consciously cross over to the spiritual echelons, the entire focus then singularly shifts to the self-actualization of one's soul that would ultimately mature only when it amalgamates with the Supreme Being. That would be everlasting.

Thus, as we mature, so does our awareness of our surroundings. Experience, introspection along with the principle of inclusive sustenance leads us to inculcate within us a sense of responsibility such that we no longer hold others responsible for any frictions or deficits. Rather we strive to fix those impediments ourselves so as to evolve at a faster pace with better visualised and controlled outcomes. Our level shifts from laying stress on the physical as well as cosmic self to the spiritual self and from self-aggrandising to absolute humility, moulding our synergetic responses accordingly. At this stage, we align with the upwardly directed vectors without falling in conflict with our surroundings.

The realisation creeps in that it is 'My work and my responsibility', so it now becomes the basis of my existence. In the process, we also learn how to keep the physical as well as the chemical balance of our body in complete confluence with each other as one would impact the other. We then gradually succeed in ascending from the lower thresholds of both our body and mind. Once we do that, we rise above our worldly constraints to become as vacuous as a hollow flute, always ready to allow free inflow of air to produce harmonious music. Thus in our liberated form, the chords of love, compassion and assimilation smoothly take over our otherwise 'self-entangled' mental states. This facilitates the higher synergy levels to charge us differently. We then understand the holistic sustenance of all our formats, that is, our physical form, our superficial mind, the deep-seated cosmic mind and the spiritual-self. Different levels enable different levels of cognitions and processors leading to varied degrees of absorption and assimilation. We are now controlled by our inner self, rather than being enslaved by any extrinsic factor. It is there that the inner vectors become stable and blissfully seamless.

The Holy scriptures and sages from various cultures also help in ultimately unfolding the mysteries of our existence that are based on years of experiential rationalities beyond the known scientific domains. It is important at this point to reiterate that the sensory led base level instincts leading to greed, lust, arrogance, ego or combination of such negative downwardly mobile vectors are to be discarded. These are to be replaced by virtues such as sharing, kindness, forgiveness, love and unconditional acceptance of the surroundings as well as the happenings in our lives. Being in the moment and giving hundred per cent focus is the only opportune possibility enabling our upwardly kinetic uplift. People experiencing life differently have evolved different ways of their upward thrust in their zeal to rise to the higher echelons. One way is to focus on a mentor or deity and assimilate energy levels in the direction shown by them. Devotional feelings are the key factors here. The other way is to focus on our energy centers or *chakras* and pierce through them one by one through "hat-yog'. The most powerful yet the easy way is the 'surat-shabd yog' with the help of resonating sound energy synthesised in a holistic pattern termed as *Naam* or *Shabad*. The process is to internalise with one's innermost self and uplift within. The experiential dispositions by Saints like 'Kabir', as elaborated earlier, speak of the 'take-off stage' and the 'meditative-stage'. [We reach the take-off stage only when negative factors are mitigated and our life becomes free of any bondages. Thereafter, an undisturbed internal focus and unhindered connect with the chord of the 'ultimate sound' will keep taking us forward from one level to the other]. Needless to say that our logical self *prima facie* won't accept this, till we really experience it within oneself. This experience overshadows any worldly logic.

I have been pondering deeply over all these facets that my father often narrated. Many of them I discovered in our holy scriptures or the discourses of our Saints, including *Kabir–Bani*. I even practiced them for short intervals. Finally, I had the good fortune of being able to attend to my mother in her old age. In the culminating last three years, she stayed with me. She had evolved over a period of time through *Satsang* and under the mentorship of my Father's maternal uncle, who as mentioned earlier was an enlightened soul. My mother who was suffering from cancer did not let that deter her. She would often pray in gratitude, "I know, all this is as per your wish in consonance with my karmic burden. I wish to express no disagreement with your 'Will'. My only appeal before you is to grant me the strength to stoically bear with it. I am now in absolute confluence with Your bliss."

After she left this world to merge with the divine, almost for a month or so I remained in an unexplainable 'magnetic field'. I practiced some of the above mentioned learnings. I then started experiencing inner actualisations in my own way. I find myself incapable of putting it into words but recommend that all should make a small beginning today and now. Your discovery within shall be your own blissful possession.

I conclude this chapter with a tale from Buddha's life. Several devotees used to visit him. One day, a rich man brought expensive gifts and a generous spread of food for him. But Buddha did not take any cognisance. Then came an old lady attired in tatters carrying a half-eaten pomegranate that was both stale and rotten. She presented that half eaten pomegranate to Buddha with absolute devotion. Gautam Buddha accepted it and ate it with zeal. One of his disciples watching the proceedings was baffled at his response and could not prevent himself from asking Buddha why he had chosen the stale pomegranate over the lavish food spread. Buddha said, "See, the rich man has parted with only a very tine fraction of his possessions which he has offered to me. On the other hand, this pious old lady who possesses only that half eaten pomegranate has offered it to me. So she has actually given her hundred per cent to me. It was that which made all the difference." If we can understand the level of elevated thought exemplified by this tale from Buddha's life, we would then have achieved our absolute confluence with divinity. What a level!

☐

7

Beliefs Form the Seeds

"If you don't sow the right seed, then wild unrestrained thoughts will anyways take over your mind, as your senses will keep constantly absorbing something or the other from the surroundings. An influx of garbage will then vitiate your system. Focus on how you can avoid it or convert it into healthy manure".

One of the popular generic dictum states: "The growth of a tree is reflected in the latent potential of its seed." While environmental factors would undoubtedly have their impact but the core characteristics cannot be undermined. From Nature's perspective, we are similar to plants but with a difference. One crucial difference is the presence of our mind which introduces dynamic and abstract mechanisms such as logic, emotions, cognition and beliefs. Among these, whereas the first three may be relevant for the operational processing by the mind, the most important vector that determines direction of our thinking is 'belief'. It trickles down from the conscious segment of the mind to the passive sub-conscious segment, based upon repetitive patterns and well engrained levels of faith. This process of 'belief' then becomes the epicenter. It procreates signals for future germination. It creates a web of instincts.

"Please go ahead and do a self-audit. Analyse your deeds. Try to identify the beliefs that prompt you to acquire a set pattern of thoughts and actions which may fuel your unwanted instincts. Also regulate your food intakes that may hamper your meditative practices." Such were the pearls of wisdom my father imbibed from his maternal uncle. He would reiterate them in his own engaging style, but it precisely meant that we should reflect and 'probe within' as a matter of daily practice. In fact, beliefs are the controllers of our responses. Hence, when something goes wrong as part of our response pattern our experienced elders and peers advise us to first focus on changing our beliefs. Unless we do that any debate on merits or demerits of a phenomenon may not leave any impact on us.

People who have evolved to a higher level of

thinking, above the common masses, are a source of learning for us. Their cumulative experience indicates that it may require concerted efforts of 'conscious-adaptation' for at least a period of a few months to bring in any consistent change in a habit. It would entail further meditative processes for extended spells in order to give it a semblance of some permanence. To facilitate the process of unlearning and relearning, some specific tools and techniques are recommended. These include interaction with persons of similar interests, self-mentoring and meditation with revived zeal.

Beliefs are, thus, the key. The process of concretization of beliefs underlines the importance of the ancient *ashram* system where the need of a mentor or *Guru*, the right associations and experience sharing are its core pillars. In this context it is also relevant to note that experiential 'demonstration-effects' are found to be more fruitful, rather than observation based discourses. Logic per-se may not be so effective. Eventually, everything falls back to one's 'thoughts'. We must, therefore, grow a nursery of virtuous thoughts by observation, learning from relevant books, imbibing good practices, and imitating the Mentor.

On other days father would advise: "If you don't sow the right seed, then wild unrestrained thoughts will anyways takeover your mind, as your senses will keep constantly absorbing something or the other from the surroundings. An influx of garbage will then vitiate your system. Focus on how you can avoid it or otherwise convert it into healthy manure."

Gradually, these teachings started getting engrained in my mind. I initially adopted a twofold approach—Firstly, I increased the time slot of meditation during my yoga session. Secondly, I started working on following a creative lifestyle that would keep both my body and mind busy with positive construct. To start with, I zeroed down on certain broad options that included–generating 'wellness' for others, accepting challenging assignments related to social upliftment and attempting to bring a smile on the faces of those around me. It soon spread to my pursuing creative hobbies that would help keep my mind cheerfully occupied with positive thoughts. The one thing I had learnt in the process is that 'everything leaves a distinct impression on our mind'.

My father had not only been a voracious reader but also believed in exchanging notes with people from all walks of life. Taking a cue from the 'genetic-modification' of a seed under laboratory conditions, he would say: "*Satsang* is the laboratory for a *Jeev*. The rigid and distorted configurations or aberrations in one's personality acquired over a period of time (over many births) are amended through a single stroke of a *Sant-Satguru*, the ultimate Mentor. We may have to struggle endlessly when we are bereft of guidance, but when under the supervision of our Guru we can achieve the same promptly. Hence, devote yourself to the teachings of the Guru and then practice them accordingly."

An unrestrained mind, the elephant within, may exploit our senses to focus on negative domains and lead us to a depraved and vitiated state of being. Hence, sages have left meaningful advisories for us in the form of lucid couplets or short stories. A routine audit of one's actions and thoughts, self-mentoring via meditation and creative indulgence in the company of true seekers or a true mentor is the crux. These issues are of paramount importance in our daily routine and they need to be recalled frequently. Real knowledge is deemed to be adequately acquired only when we are in control of the 'animal' within us. The instinctive responses of an externalized mind, chasing pseudo pleasures seeking gratification of our base instincts, needs a total recheck and complete revamp.

At times, the question of individual morality is also raised. Simplistic morality is like water, which in different people acquires the shape of the urn it is poured in. However, when a good belief system is in place, values don't get compromised. Nevertheless, across various cultures and awareness levels, the same thing could be explained differently, ranging from written norms to well configured rituals with a clear-cut set of do's and don'ts. The crucial aspect is to see the rationale and the relevance of how things get communicated, reinforced and frozen. Once a true seeker understands 'Why', he will find out 'What' and 'How' on his own. Kabir questioned people's belief based on distorted religiosity and drew their focus beyond the cosmic zone to higher levels of spirituality.

Psycho-behavioural analysts assert that a person behaves in a particular way because he cannot behave otherwise. This premise, in fact, leads us to the core of our beliefs. Unless the core undergoes a change, the signals emanating from it won't change. Hence, the system shall keep responding accordingly. Even if we put external pressure of fear or introduce an incentive, there is no guarantee of continuity of such behaviour. On the contrary, when we simultaneously also apply the tools of behavioural change, we stand a better chance of succeeding.

The power of belief is often explained by the example of an elephant, and the method followed to tame him. When a baby elephant is kept chained for a long duration, he gradually becomes conditioned to staying that way. Then one day the chain is removed, but by then he is so conditioned that he still behaves as if he is tied and does not stray. The example is only indicative and raises more questions. My father and I often argued on this count. Shouldn't beliefs be monitored since childhood? Isn't there a need for effective parenting and primary schooling? Why such conditioning or training not given priority in India?

And my father's response would be, "Yes, that ought to be an ideal scenario. But the beauty of life is that you can restart from anywhere and relearn."

However, later on he did concede that "All this is easier said than done. It requires dedication and unceasing efforts, but surely the labour would be worth it. However to reach the ideal destination one must follow the right direction without which even the most sincere efforts will not bear fruit. Hence make a resolve early and nurture it so that the orchard of your life flourishes and bears fruit. This process will nurture humility within you and obliterate your ego. You are then free to traverse freely and nothing would be holding you back."

The most positive trait of my father was that he had utmost 'belief' in his *Guru* (spiritual mentor). The will of the 'Guru' is supreme. An old folklore explain this concept in a nutshell. An emperor took out a pearl and asked his close associates to attempt to break it. The first said, "Oh such a precious pearl! How can I even think of breaking it?" Emperor rewarded him and then called for the next one. So, one by one, each one of them came and praised the pearl but refused to break it. Each one was rewarded with gold and ornaments. Finally the emperor called his most trusted friend and requested that he should break the pearl. The friend promptly did so. All in the court murmured, "What has he done? Such a precious pearl has been destroyed!" The friend then replied, "For me the pearl is not important, but the order of the emperor is." The Emperor then rose to his feet and embraced him!

□

8

'Marination' Matters

'Pakavat' underscores the implicit faith we have in what we undertake and that we use the correct tools and tactics to do so effectively. We need to ensure that we do not regress but stay optimally committed towards an upward mobility on that well-chosen path.

"Marination is the process of soaking foods in a seasoned, often acidic, liquid before cooking". It appropriately describes the message of this chapter as it results in maturing the object which is marinated. The 'object' here is we ourselves and once immersed in the 'marinade' provided by our mentor, we become tender and tough at the same time, get cooked (pakavat) adding the flavours of spirituality, making us evolved beings who are destined to merge with the divine.

Dheere dheere re mana,
Dheere sab kuchh hoye;
Maali seenche sau ghada,
Ritu aaye phal hoye!

"*Pakavat Jaroori hai*", my father would always state with much conviction in his local dialect. He meant that we need to reach a certain level of maturity or evolution. For this, our thoughts and concepts have to stabilise and become part of an auto response in order to pass the test of *Pakavat*. It would also entail absolute clarity and confidence in the thoughts that we nurture. Though he originally meant it in the context of spiritual practices, the principle is applicable to any activity that calls for concerted drive and effort. This could apply to a routine chore such as driving a vehicle or the complex process of focusing on traversing the path of wisdom in one's life. *Pakavat* underscores the implicit faith we have in what we undertake and that we use the correct tools and tactics to do so effectively. We need to ensure that we do not regress but stay optimally committed towards an upward mobility on that well-chosen path.

The process of *Pakavat* is also dependent on the dimensions of 'time' as well as 'form'. A very popular couplet of Kabir is often cited to describe this process:

Dheere dheere re mana,
Dheere sab kuchh hoye;
Maali seenche sau ghada,
Ritu aaye phal hoye!

It means that the process of things 'maturing'

is gradual. Hence, tune your mind to appreciate and accept the process of marination. The vectors of time and form are of crucial importance. For example even if a gardener irrigates the tree with copious amounts of water, it will bear fruit only when it has matured and is ready.

This brings us back to a very important feature of Creation, which is the process of marination. With whatever little understanding of Nature we have evolved or absorbed through our sensory capabilities, we by now know for certain that Nature is holistic and intertwined. Through preliminary observation we have learnt that flora & fauna, wildlife, the environment, the earth's landscape consisting of hills, valleys, rivers and plains, are interlinked by a cause and effect relationship. They are the forces which ensure stable growth, and self-restorative properties of nature's sub-systems. While these properties and forces of Nature follow laid-down principles, they are so seamless that they appear to be in auto mode. Undue interference or imposing artificially-controlled conditions would only give way to distortions, displacements or imbalances. And that too will eventually follow a time pattern. If this is the intertwined pattern at this level, the holistic nature of divinity at the highest level is beyond anybody's comprehension!

The concept of marination is the 'key' to life. All sages have focused on a balanced approach to life with a fine sense of proportion. It can also be understood in terms of what Gautam Buddha propounded as the 'middle path'. We must pay heed to this approach, as it affects the process and its parameters. Marination via family and community influence vis-à-vis the option of complete renunciation have been well analyzed on experiential yardsticks by saints. For ordinary people the balanced path through the former option has been well recommended. The reasons are well elaborated at relevant places.

My mother used to make very good '*Kanji*' which happened to be my father's favorite. It needed to be kept out in the sun initially for a few days with certain vegetables and herbs soaked in it. *Kaanji* would then mature by a slow and natural heating process to produce the desired properties, aroma and taste. No technique to accelerate this process could compress the time required for this 'marination' to happen. In our family, *Kaanji* became synonymous with marination.

Coming to the varied facets of life, we all undergo the process of maturity whether in family relationships, job environment, social influences or political processes. When it comes to leadership influences in any of these domains, marination would imply being a patient listener, capable of evolving a combined vision, communicating effectively, creating positive demonstration effects, leading by example, being a visionary, a risk optimiser, handling perceptions and influence systems effectively. This is true of all worldly situations.

An example of Lukman is cited to highlight how beautifully he marinated himself with the thoughts, values and beliefs of his mentor to emerge as a perfect disciple. Once Lukman's mentor offered him a watermelon. His mentor was slicing pieces of the fruit himself and offering it to Lukman with obvious affection. Lukman kept eating it with increasing contentment. Observing this for some time the mentor thought that he should also have one bite at least to see how tasty the fruit was. When he took a morsel, he found the fruit to be extremely bitter. Upset he reprimanded Lukman that why he had not told him so. Instead he actually appeared to be enjoying it. Lukman said, "I was not focusing on the fruit. I was merely absorbing the love and concern in your effort."

So, spiritual advancement is an 'internalisation-process'. One needs to focus within, with a deep sense of gratitude. This marination process further calls for continuous soul searching and identifying one's shortcomings on the grid of kindness, forgiveness and patience with a view to synergising them further. Needless to say that the negative vectors of greed, lust, selfishness, jealousy and ego need to be fairly neutralised much before they vitiate our process of internalisation. Marination is not merely the absence of negative vectors, but the surfeit of the positive vectors as well. The law of nature works on the basis of the vectors that we imbibe or renounce. Once we marinate completely, it is easy to establish a connection with the pure energy levels within us. As the sages articulate, the resonance of the sound coming from the epicenter of the 'ultimate consciousness' pulls us towards it, providing the necessary upward thrust. We then elevate our levels one step after the other. Each level has its own marination process. We accordingly keep relocating ourselves on the divine grid.

What I could understand from the experience sharing with my father and what I have depicted here may not be the absolute truth. After all, we all are mere seekers. But it definitely gives us some direction and defines a road map for internalisation.

□

9

Synergy is the Key

In case of human beings the synergy is far beyond mere coherent or well networked functioning. If we were to list them, it could emerge as follows—unbounded internal levels of commitment and visualisations, demonstration effects of internalised leadership, compassionate teamwork and passionate collaborative drive. All combined in an optimum format could produce tremendous results.

As children we were explained the meaning of synergy by narrating a tale of a father and his five sons. The father gave a single stick of wood to each of his sons and asked them to break it. They all did so easily. Then he took another set of similar sticks, bound them together and again asked each one to break the bundle. Expectedly, all of them failed. Thus, as our father would explain that when combined together, the strength and impact of any object or element or a group of people is far greater than when in an isolated state. "Synergy exists at the heart of creative cooperation. It means that the whole is greater than the sum of its parts". As we grew, we realised that each person's individual output would be far less than when we work in unison. So, when one worked as a coordinated team, with zeal and a healthy competitive spirit, one could achieve far more than on one's own. This extra outcome was the result of synergy.

However, the story of invisible multipliers doesn't conclude here. Our father elaborated: "It is imperative that we attend *Satsang*. Multiple people assemble there and collectively listen to spiritual discourses, discuss their relevance and then deliberate upon the teaching, assimilating them through meditative practices." This was our father's way to motivate us in our younger days to attend *Satsang sessions*! "Right values, right thinking, right attitude will ensure that you stay on the right track," he constantly asserted. On occasions of significance, a *Bhandara* was also organised. *Bhandara* is an event where all the devotees conglomerate and share food served as *Prasad* (which is first offered to the deity and then taken as a token of His blessings). All the attendees serve each other.

With such beginnings, as we grew up we started grasping the term 'synergy' in different contexts that could range from machine synergy to human synergy,

from local synergy to National synergy, from synergy of physical elements to the spiritual synergy.

When various components of a machine sync together under a given system or process, the output increases to its optimal level. Similar is the case with teams working together. However, in case of human beings the synergy is far beyond mere coherent or well-networked functioning. If we were to list them, it could emerge as follows--unbounded internal levels of commitment and visualisations, demonstration effects of internalised leadership, compassionate teamwork and passionate collaborative drive. All combined in an optimum format could produce tremendous results. A perfect synergy could also have its by-products that may open new vistas for advancement. There is no mathematical logic in it. It is experiential and depends on a fine combination of various vectors at a given point of time. Here the role of leadership becomes very critical: leading by example to being equal amongst all; knowing the people you connect with even better than their own mothers; setting meaningful goals with powerful strategies through a process of shared vision; being a facilitator and helping people to succeed and becoming their mentor as does a mother.

"Even if you fail, so what, you are still my child. We shall strive harder and succeed next time," is how a mother assures her children with an ownership based emotionality. So the art of making everyone a stakeholder and carrying them along does wonders and gives very positive results.

As we go up the ladder in our work life then socio-political architecture, national interest, local and regional synergy, cultural confluences, economic optimality—all these domains start occupying our mental space. We see society and the nation as bigger units of sustenance. The idea of enlisting all these perspectives is to drive home a critical point that inclusivity and collaborative awareness is an essential condition for any synergetic outcome.

We did realise through our worldly experience that physical and mental energy levels could be combined in multiple ways to get on to much higher and effective levels of sustenance, in terms of work output level as well as the quotient of acceptance in the environment. While striving to carve a place for oneself, we also realised that much would depend on the level of our skills and humility.

A folklore illustrates the importance of synergy within, in order to generate synergy outside. A lady took her child to a saint and requested him to ask her child not to eat too many sweets. The saint told the lady to come after a week. When the lady visited him again after a week along with her son, the saint merely told the child, "Son, don't eat too many sweets." He then asked the lady to take her son back. The lady was perplexed and offended, "If you had to tell my child only this, then why did you make me wait for a week." The saint smiled and said, "That was because till last week I was consuming too many sweets myself. I asked you to come later as then I gave them up myself practicing what I was going to preach." The story ends with a strong message of synergy with one's purpose and character.

By the time we developed our perspective on these formats, my father had moved on to, "Enough of worldly indulgences, now grow spiritually within." And each time I met him or interacted on phone, I was reminded of this point and this alone. When gradually introduced to yogic routines and spiritual way of life, our entire perception underwent a change. We now began to understand the mind and body in a different format. We learnt how each 'power-point' in our body could be invoked. The third dimension of 'Faith' and the consequent connect with the spiritual-self was intriguing and miraculous. I could not comprehend it properly in the beginning. But with constant persuasion from my father, my disposition gradually began to undergo a change. There now arose possibilities of deeper internalisation. The new observations generated a wholesome visualization of life and a fresh flow of energy. The new elevations enabled me to be least perturbed or impacted by the factors that were earlier manifesting as major road blocks. The complete alignment of body, mind and spirit was now producing enhanced positive synergies with a new sense of bliss within. As per Saints, so important is the human form that even when deities or sages need to spiritually elevate further, they need to come back to the 'human work station'. Hence, they repeatedly assert not to waste this rare opportunity.

For a complete yogic experience that enables the total alignment of body, mind and soul; sub-yoga in the form of *asana* plays an integral role in shaping the 'new being', as spinal alignment is equally important for unhindered energy flows. Right from preparing for the take-off stage to upward mobility is a unique 'absorption within' that has to be experienced and cannot be described by words alone. Each moment brings with it a profound awareness of the Creator. Connecting with the surroundings also brings you closer to the 'grace' of the Creator. Certain cosmic waves already exist in one's surroundings. We can tune our human system like a machine to gel with the frequency of these eternal wavelengths and absorb them. The logic is simple. One needs to attempt it to realise it.

Synergy, that needs to be understood in all its facets, is the key. It would remain relevant throughout, beginning from the primitive facets of life to its culminating level.

□

10

Our need for a Mentor

A mentor is valued for his experiential guidance. We must lay focus on his guidance and accordingly internalise. Our respect for the mentor should be absolute but we need to refrain from ritualistic worship as it would do nothing except lead us into a state of redundancy.

Why do we need a mentor? This is the most critical question which we need to address. Many of us might find the idea unnecessary and assume oneself to be capable of finding the way ahead on one's own. However, experience clearly shows that a meaningful life is not possible without proper guidance, whatsoever be the arena of our life: it could be our personal life, work life, community sustenance; our physical growth, mental evolvement

Sadhu aisa chahiye, jaisa saop subhay
Saar saar ko gahi rahe, thotha dei uday!

or spiritual advancement. What could be the plausible reasons? Is it that the mentor has already undergone a variety of experiences, already having traversed the path we are now aspiring to take or has already reached the destination successfully? Is it that we, in order to keep ourselves disciplined, need some control or guidance? Is it that the mentor provides a balcony view that is essential in order to have an unbiased validation? Or is it that amidst the array of confusions and diverging tides during the course of our life, we need an anchor? Can it be that we constantly need an observer and coach for course correction? Is it that we need a motivator, who can clear our doubts and inject more mental or emotional synergies, and last but not the least, is it the fear of the unknown that prompts us to look for a spiritual mentor?

My father had implicit faith in his maternal uncle (we addressed him as Babuji), so for all practical purposes he was his sole mentor, be it with respect to worldly issues or spiritual. During those days to communicate one needed to express one's thoughts via a postcard or an inland letter and thus father would receive replies from Babuji. Thereafter, he would need no further deliberations. The amount of confidence he had in Babuji, gave him adequate mental strength to follow his guidelines and define his own path. My father was convinced that Babuji would have first taken a thorough balcony view before responding. Babuji, given his virtuous life style as well as his close connection with his *Guru*, was bestowed with deep spiritual enlightenment. Everyone in our family was aware of this.

My mother was not very well-educated and had received very basic education. She belonged to a time when women kept personal issues to themselves and would not discuss them outside close family members. At best they would share personal issues with their mother in law, their sisters or at most with very close friends. While she had lived a protected life with limited exposure to the outside world, but like my father, she too had implicit faith in Babuji. He had written many books based on the discourses of his *Guru* whom he had personally served in the capacity of the personal assistant. Hence, whenever mother needed guidance she would peruse through a few leaves of his book, and based on the gist of its message connect it with her present circumstances and address the issue at hand. This would be followed by a session of meditative praying and the ensuing thoughts that came to her mind became her guiding factor.

As per a folklore, a competition was held between two disciples. They were given two parallel stone walls to work on. The first one decorated that wall with enthusiasm and to the best of his capabilities. The second just kept rubbing the stone walls repeatedly till it developed a sheen giving its surface a mirror like effect. When the walls were uncovered for evaluation, the reflection of the decorated wall on the polished wall was miraculous. That is how a mother reflects her divinity as a mentor merely by shining from within, even though she herself may not possess the art of creating beauty. The magnitude of her unfettered glory manifests its effect constantly.

Now between these absolute options we also have several variations. We may not get a perfect mentor for all times or for all our needs. That means we may need to have a mentor as per our level of maturity. Then personal and professional life may demand different mentors for different spheres of our life. But whatever it be, the ultimate truth remains unchanged which is that, getting an able mentor will render us supreme happiness and this can be seen in most of the 'successful and contended' people around us. If, you were to ask me, I would emphatically assert that a mentor is critical for all the recommendations that we have listed at the onset.

'Learning' is a unique phenomenon. With so many diverse sources of learning with their sub-optimal perspectives, our learnings often become distorted. Thus the question arises; how do we successfully imbibe the flow of inputs that we receive through life? They need to be processed through our 'hardware' and 'software', that is, our body and mind to make them an integral part of our auto-response mechanism. With a mentor we not only condition our body and mind for an upward thrust, but also upgrade the overall operating environment. There is no doubt that a mentor creates a huge demonstration effect but only if he or she has achieved the desired level of perfection in his or her own lifestyle.

Besides granting complete clarity on the various opaque and confusing phenomena in life, a mentor also assumes the responsibility of a good communicator. Communication between the mentor and mentee goes beyond merely the verbal and visual communication for transfer of knowledge but also the intrinsic exchange of wisdom which is absorbed and retained by the mentee, at the same level of intensity as desired by the sender. One has to watch against likely distortions, displaced silent or ulterior communication which the mind registers and gets subjugated by its negative implications without any forewarning. Hence, a good mentor always keeps reminding the mentee, 'What is your purpose of learning?'

If we enter the sublime zone of human sustenance, the complete alignment of body, mind and spirit presents a different landscape than what we see in aggregation of the three components separately. Since a human being is a 'synergetic entity', it is advisable to understand the human machine and its responses in terms of yogic assimilation of these three elements of our being. As we mature, we learn to differentiate between the human self, cosmic self and the spiritual self. As soon as we realise this, the whole approach to life changes. We tend to become far more aware, inclusive as well as responsive. We tend to neutralise our superficial mind and internalise to connect with our inner core. Our inner core or the soul or 'surat' then integrates beyond the forces of nature with the divine link that is all pervasive. With the passage of time, this deep learning then further leads to many intuitive predictions.

We have understood 'artificial intelligence' and its predictive capabilities in the context of machines without realising that our body system in itself is the best machine that the Creator has devised and our inner core has inherent, faultless predictive capabilities. However, this requires extensive internalization of our learnings in a similar manner as we hone machine learning through repeated programming. In the same way, we need a mentor to programme us well. In his absence the smallest mistakes could severely regress our progress and the 'opportunity cost' could be too high for us to restore *status-quo-ante*. Hence, once we have risen to the higher echelons, a mentor becomes indispensable.

My father deciphered these learnings by rising to a higher level of understanding of life. For him, devotion to the spiritual being was the biggest driving force. He would often say: "If you are able to attain progress on this spiritual path, you will no longer need to worry about the worldly issues. The largest value quotient of spirituality will take care of all your other lower cravings; you shall gain both, *Deen* (Divine) as well as *Duniya* (world). But if you are only submerged in yearning for worldly attractions, you will be left with nothing." In whatever sense he said it, it unfolded the ultimate truth that for blissful external sustenance, one has to traverse to the highest level of spiritual existence that governs the whole Creation.

Sadhu aisa chahiye, jaisa soop subhay
Saar saar ko gahi rahe, thotha dei uday!

"The *Sadhu* (*Guru* or Mentor) is like a winnowing pan that retains the core grain and discards the husk or the unwanted." Thus, focus is laid on the 'right mentor' who can guide us well. Searching for a complete *Guru* is the first challenge. A mentor with no vision cannot show us the way. Those who have attained spiritual 'moksha' further insist that the mentor should be a contemporary who is aligned with our present life. This is similar to the way a medic who is practicing in the present setting alone can diagnose the medical condition of our body and prescribe the necessary medicine. The doctor must accurately diagnose the illness and prescribe specifically for the patient in question. A mentor constantly watching our progress and modulating the practices or controlling any distractions is *sine-quo-non*. What do we do then if we fail to discover a worthy mentor? The experiential response is that we need to rely upon a person who is more enlightened than us but the search for a worthy mentor should nevertheless continue. In a relatively dynamic scenario, there is no scope for either stagnating at one juncture or finding refuge in some ritual or standard procedures. Constant review and self-evaluation, mentor-consultation, internalisation and refinement of our thoughts are the best methods for the desired ascent to higher echelons. It is reiterated that one could pay a heavy price for any lapse on our part at this juncture of ascendancy, as we could get pulled down to a state far worse than where we had started initially. Hence, the guiding and watchful hand of a mentor is vital.

Once we decide upon a mentor, our faith in him needs to remain unshaken and resolute. This is essential, else the mind may question his guidance, nor would we practice his teaching with absolute adherence and devotion. This will be a serious handicap resulting in our giving less than our full potential, which will result in failure. Our respect for the mentor should be absolute but we need to refrain from ritualistic worship, else it would do nothing except lead us to a state of redundancy. I end with a simple *Jatak Katha* (folk lore) on 'why we need a mentor in real time'. A businessman while dying told his son, "Please ensure that you go to work at the shop in the shadows and return in the shadows too." The dutiful son followed his father's advice and built a canopied path running all the way from his home to the shop. In the bargain he ended up investing an exorbitant sum of money in building it and thus his business was doomed at its very onset. He was furious and faulted his father for ruining him. Desperate, he approached a mentor. The mentor explained, "Well, your father had given the correct advice, but you understood it wrongly." What he meant was that every day you should go to your shop before the sun is up and return only when it is dusk. What he wanted was for you to work hard with honesty and dedication." This simple anecdote says it all about the blunders we may commit that would adversely change the course and direction of our life.

□

11

Hunger for Learning

These pearls of wisdom coming from Vishvakarma, a simple man of meagre means made me feel like a dwarf before him. That moment I realised his true worth. For him, I was his Master. But that day, he became my 'Guru'. This episode greatly impacted my thinking and values. This is a profound example of a powerful demonstration effect emanating from a ground level humble practitioner. Materially, I was much richer than him. But spiritually, when I compared myself with him, he proved to be a giant far richer than me.

They say: "There is a Guru at every door step for a true seeker." It may sound like truism but it's underlying message is deep. I too did not pay much heed to it until I underwent an experience that changed my entire life. A person used to work at our house performing odd jobs. A very simple and gentle

man from a rural background. Not very sharp but very loyal. His name was 'Vishvakarma'. On every holiday or on festivals or when some guests came visiting us, a special meal would be cooked to celebrate the occasion. As part of the culture of our family, these special dishes were also offered to all the help in the house. However, 'Vishvakarma' would politely refuse to accept them. Initially, we did not insist. Then, out of sheer curiosity, I started observing what he ate. I found that after finishing his daily chores, he would go to the backyard and cook some lentil in a pan. His method of cooking too was very basic. He would use four bricks to make a *chulha* and wood chips to build a fire. Once the wood would turn to charcoal, he would bake a potato or brinjal in the charcoal and then roast a few *chapatis* in it. That was all that his frugal meal comprised of. One day, I insisted that he too should partake of the special dishes that had been cooked in the house. When he resisted, then I worked on him emotionally, coaxing him to divulge why he was so averse to accepting our offerings. He finally blurted: "Saab, I don't wish to offend you. I am truly grateful to you and honour your feelings. I know for sure that as long as I am in your service and under your care, I would enjoy this special treatment and delicious food. But after you leave, I will have to fall back on my own meagre means." I countered showing some impatience and said: "So what, God will surely make some other way ahead for you." His subsequent reply left me speechless, "Saab, once I start eating this food provided by you, my tongue will get habituated to it and my body will demand more of the same. And once you are gone, I will be denied this indulgence. This is then likely to either make me miserable or to compromise my integrity. I am scared of falling in that trap. I am afraid where that temptation would eventually take me and how deeply it would annihilate my self-esteem."

These pearls of wisdom coming from Vishvakarma a simple man of meagre means made me feel like a dwarf before him. That moment I realised his real true worth. For him, I was his Master. But that day, he became my *Guru*. This episode greatly impacted my thinking and values. This is a profound example of the powerful demonstration effect emanating from a ground level humble practitioner. Materially, I was much richer than him. But spiritually, when I compared myself with him, he proved to be a giant far richer than me.

Having cited the above example, I would like to carry you back to the experiential narrations of my father. He always encouraged meetings with everyone, people from all walks of life and earnestly listened to their stories. Then he would quickly highlight the critical aspects and their relevance. He also read many books and correlated various depictions made by learned characters from across various cultures and timelines. He would visit places to confirm various premises that would have emerged in his mind from diverse readings and discussions. Ultimately, it would boil down to the vicissitudes of one's life, the process of emancipation and identification of gainful spirituality that one needed to identify and then hone. (So would any great leader in an organisation or those at the helm of affairs for the best intrinsic benefit of the people they lead).

Like Eklavya, my father too would observe his mentor (Babuji) and try to emulate him. However, at times, my mother would say, "You are emulating his response patterns, but have you brought in the required changes within your heart to sustain those learnings?" This threw open the question of worthiness. Mere changing of the outer cover would not serve any real purpose or give results. In that context my mother provided him with a detailed balcony view of himself. She would cite as examples the profound humility of two devotees, who hailed from a remote village of Uttar Pradesh, and would laboriously carry water from a considerable distance every day in order to fill the bath of their mentor. This was because of their absolute devotion and sense of a self-imposed *sewa* (service). In the process they actually happened to serve other devotees too. And their best virtue was that they always maintained a stoic silence with no hostile reaction whatever be the provocation. A few folks gave them derisive looks and passed sardonic comments for performing such a menial service. However, what needs to be noted is the sense of satisfaction that overcame them. It was exclusively theirs and intrinsic to them. Nobody could rob them of that blissful experience. They stood enriched far beyond those who had cast derogatory aspersions at them.

Another insightful anecdote that my father related to his friends goes as follows. "A saint was sitting alongside a river. He noticed a scorpion being swept away by the current of the river struggling to escape the torrent. The saint's instinct was to try and pick it up in order to save it. The moment he would lift the scorpion out of the water on to his palm, the scorpion would sting him. Obviously, the saint's natural reaction was to jerk and pull back his hand and as a result the scorpion would fall back into the water. The saint would then immediately pick the scorpion up again. This process was repeated multiple times. A curious passer-by was intrigued by the saint's persistence in attempting to save the scorpion. He could not resist inquiring why the saint was trying to save the scorpion inspite of the scorpion stinging him repeatedly. The saint looked up and with a broad benign smile across his face remarked, "Look, when this scorpion is refusing to give up its habit, why should I give up mine." This is an old 'folklore', yet extremely relevant in today's times as it is equally applicable to a leader as well as a mentor, both of whom need to set examples and lead their followers from the front.

Our life is nothing but a series of experiences. No two situations are ever exactly the same. Dynamism demands keen observation and integrated learning. Each new layer of 'realisation' in life helps us to rise up further. The externalities however remain the same. With studied marination we gradually discover and transform ourselves from within and rise to higher levels where our perspectives, emotions and virtues all undergo a dramatic change. We become more inclusive and self-responsive. We begin to discover a sense of unadulterated peace and gradually eliminate all those triggers that are the stimulants for conflicts within us. Every moment then has something unique to offer. Those who have gained this realisation, actually evolve with every single breath that they take. The quest for a better version of oneself, knowing that we are limited only by ourselves, thus holds the key. For a seeker, his hunger for learning is perpetual. There is no stopping it till eternity.

□

12

Negativity paves the way for Positivity

The purpose of discussing negativity from all perspectives is to bring home the point that in this cosmos negativity goes hand in hand with positivity. However, our internal bliss is contingent on positivity. Accordingly, we must be prepared for negativity and look for options within it to discover an opportunity that would eventually facilitate our arriving at positivity. Human being living in the kinetic form have to encounter negative as well as positive dimensions every day.

Experiences in life indicate that all success models have emerged as a consequence of what they have learnt from failure. Initially, failure is the likely outcome. Success emerges only after the failures teach us to imbibe refined combinations of positive factors workable at that given point of time. Positive thinking to optimistic visualisations, synergetic alignment to integration of all sub-systems, a hundred per cent commitment from within and an all-inclusive approach have been found to be the success mantras. My father repeatedly asserted that clarity of direction, honest intentions and consistent efforts should be in place, which means, one needs to put in one's hundred percent to succeed. In fact, failures are likely during our initial attempts but the experience that you derive in the process, actually motivates you to discover your final model of success. That is the light that you are able to discover only at the end of the tunnel. (My father belonged to Ajmer district of Rajasthan, so he often cited the example of the seventeen attempts that were made by Mahmud of Ghazni to win the Taragarh fort).

We are put to the real test only when under the influence of negativity. Like the glitter of gold, that emerges only after it has undergone treatment by fire so shall we shine after being submitted to the furnace of life. Life also teaches us how hard and when to strike for success just like a blacksmith must strike when the iron is hot. Challenges that we have to face in life and the negative forces that surround us actually help to shape our true selves and prepare us for success. Those who have not fallen, will not

know how to rise. But the essential condition, there too, is to be resilient and have the will to fight back. Then the entire universe comes together to support us. This is the core law of Nature.

So whether going by scientific or spiritual explanations, we have learnt that simple friction or desire had caused the Big Bang. The potential consciousness or energy, while being kinetic, segregates into negative and positive polarities. Religions say that 'Satan' or 'Devil', a symbol of negativity, was shunted out of heaven and thus began the process of Creation. Scientifically, centrifugal and centripetal forces kept operating on each other to form different gradients of energy. This initial discussion gives us a frame to start with and the point to grasp here is the indispensability of negative polarity in the whole process of creation.

Behavioral motivators tell us, "When one door closes, another opens!" This dictum has much to convey to us. The world is in a dynamic state and constantly changing with nothing being static. Neither the pains, nor the pleasures! Hence, negativity has to be succeeded or accompanied by positivity.

In fact, those who have tasted success in the real sense, realise the value of adversity. A crisis actually offers an opportunity to shine and evolve further. In fact, negativity provides the background, where positivity shines and both are part of the dynamic process. Thus, we find that there is a learning curve effect here too.

Sages and saints have written about their experiences and revelations as to how they have evolved by undergoing negative experiences to become positive personalities. The bondages of the world themselves become instrumental in liberating you. This is a very interesting phenomenon.

"Bandhan se bandhan katen, Nirbandh hojaye"

(Bondages shall be neutralised by bondages alone to eventually liberate you: Santmat)

The purpose of discussing negativity from all perspectives is to bring home the point that in the cosmos negativity goes hand in hand with positivity. However, our internal bliss is contingent upon positivity. Accordingly, we must be prepared for negativity and look for options within it to discover an opportunity that would eventually facilitate our arriving at positivity. Human being living in the kinetic form have to encounter negative as well as positive dimensions every day. While the following anecdote was cited by a saint in the spiritual context, it can be understood in context of our own worldly goals or passion. The saint was asked what do you do when a happy event crosses your door step. His reply was, "I ask that 'pleasant event' to wait as I introspect before my deity. If I get an affirmative reply, I welcome it, else I let it go." This was followed by the second question, "And what do you do if any sorrow or negativity passes your doorstep?" His prompt reply was, "I run to the door and welcome it as each negativity brings me closer to my deity and becomes a stimulus for me to try even harder." This has not only far reaching spiritual connotations but is also applicable in the management of our worldly affairs. Successful leaders welcome adversity as it offers them an opportunity to evolve and thereby redefine and focus their performance which would lead them to become more refined and confident beings. Each failure makes them better prepared for the future and in turn generates improved capacities in their team or organisation. Facing negativity, identifying the positivity in it, and then converting that negativity into positivity is the hallmark of an ultimate winner. Negativity is extremely volatile resulting in a downward thrust, while positivity gives an upward thrust, nurturing blissful stability. In our turbulent dynamic environment, it is the accepted way of life. Those who have made it a new normal in their mind and spirit have successfully discovered the long-term business of positivity. But those who experience positivity but are unable to sustain the virtuous cycle may stagnate and lose it just as fast, and get trapped in a vicious circle of negativity. This took me several years to understand and adopt accordingly in life. Once you learn the art of welcoming negativity and processing it into an opportunity, you assume the status of a good swimmer who is no more bothered by the incoming tide or the consequent rising water level as he is confident that he will manage to swim across successfully. As he internalizes he then puts himself on a different pedestal and moves ahead. The higher the pedestal the higher the energy of our engines. You may find it tiresome to carry heavy baggage, but once you have boarded a train or a plane, it now carries the burden for you. The baggage then no longer remains your headache. Hence adverse situations impel you to seek better platforms, better engines and better drivers of 'life'.

The spiritual experience prompts us to believe that relativity is the hallmark of the cosmic domain amidst the flow of negativity and positivity, amidst illusions and the truth. Successfully traversing through this domain will then provide us with the opportunity to attain a state of absolute purity and humility. This will eventually enable us to integrate with the ultimate 'Consciousness'.

□

13

Spiritual Seekers

Having evolved thus, the spiritual seeker repeatedly practices the principle of 'letting go'. For him, death is the doorway to a higher assimilation of divinity. There is now no fear. There is only an unbounded eagerness to attain higher levels of an all-enveloping bliss. He or she, therefore, remains unaffected by any worldly upheavals that are otherwise perceived as threats by a commoner. They are no longer insecure. They know how to swim across, irrespective of the depth of the water.

Spirituality is an intrinsic dimension of the entire creation. It is the inner alignment of our body, mind and soul with the epicenter of absolute consciousness. Where our body is governed by our senses that are capable of connecting us to the external environment, it is the mind that does the

internal processing. Without going into basics, it is adequate to underscore the point that spirituality starts beyond the realms of one's body and mind. A spiritual seeker goes beyond the limitations of the body and mind to locate higher energy levels of perpetual sustenance. A spiritual seeker, therefore, is adept at invoking higher energy levels. He doesn't fight his battle based on the acquisition of mere material resources or on chuffing his 'ego' or creating malicious manoeuvers or manipulating to gain coercive controls. On the contrary, he neutralizes his mind and turns the focus away from his bodily form by firmly positioning himself at the seat of his soul, his conscience. His tools are inclusiveness, kindness, ability to pardon, gratitude and love. He logs on to the inner current that connects him to the divine source. In such a state his whole perspective changes. His presence and participation invokes positive energy and acceptance from within. He consequently experiences and absorbs the divinity around. The laws of attraction and creation facilitate the spiritual warrior to constantly evolve in a purer format. Such assimilative and blissful persona are rare to come by. Such people are far removed from all the negative characteristics like anger, coercion and manipulations, they create their own space and exude a positive aura that makes things happen. I am reiterating these negative tools such as jealousy, anger, revenge and egoistical posturing, as most of us fall prey to them which consequently invokes suffering. Thus we become losers right from the beginning. These negative energies, even if they initially provide a false feeling of elation, are not sustainable and eventually will lead to our drowning into an abyss of negativity and self-pity. The experiences of sages as well as those remembered for their virtuous contributions in taking humanity ahead are enough to substantiate this point.

Carrying this further, my father would elaborate, "Being a spiritual seeker, you shall achieve the divine and through Him the necessary resources in this world. Whatever is due to you will come to you anyways. No enemy, no evil can succeed in preventing it from happening." As my mentor, he succeeded in giving me the confidence to start building my spiritual base too.

Our scriptures, while discussing the lives of spiritual seekers, mention that such souls also, like the common man, indulge in worldly acts and yet remain unaffected. They have actually evolved to the level where they can of their own accord and will, ascend up the divine ladder. Attaining such a state is difficult but not impossible. The base line is to first let the 'ego' go. The soul within us then realizes how serious we are. The inner vibrations that then begin to emerge are so potent that all the facilitating virtues of being inclusive, truthful, kind, humble and deep appreciation of the benefits received *suo-moto* freely flow within us.

The perspective of such seekers is to assimilate in the divine flow that is not bound by time, space or form. The initial invocation facilitating the upwardly kinetic state through merger with the *Naam* (the power of sound) eventually leads them to assimilate with the divine element that now emerges in its original form.

Having evolved thus, the spiritual warrior repeatedly practices the principle of 'letting go'. For him, death is the doorway to a higher assimilation of divinity. There is now no fear. There is only an unbounded eagerness to attain higher levels of an all-enveloping bliss. He or she, therefore, remains unaffected by any worldly upheavals that are otherwise perceived as threats by a commoner. They are no longer insecure. They know how to swim across, irrespective of the depth of the water. These warriors, though following the rules of body sustenance, in fact sustain at a much higher energy level. Here I would like to mention two references from earlier saints; one from Soordas:

Man ko jite khada rahe
Wo balihari Soor!

(One who can win over the mind, is the real warrior)

And the other from Kabir:

Ye chadar sur nur muni odhi;
Odh ke mailee keeni;
Das Kabir jatan se odhi,
Jyon ki tyon dhar deen!

(All including the seers and Gods came into this world in the pure body form but could not keep it free of taint and impurities. However, an honest devotee, so asserts Kabir, lives life consciously and sparingly and finally departs from his worldly existence without tarnishing or obscuring its purity.)

A spiritual warrior draws a bigger line adjacent to those that reflect our worldly desires, such that the latter now appear insignificant. Thus, without being in conflict with the illusionary surroundings of this world, he elevates himself to the higher echelons successfully ascending the spiritual ladder.

□

About the Inspirator

Born on 10th December, 1931, late Prem Sukh Maheshwari hailed from a small town Kishangarh in Ajmer distt of Rajasthan (India). Brought up amidst scarcities, he learnt to brace himself to face the challenges in his life. Later on he moved to Agra to pursue higher studies under the mentorship of his maternal uncle late Babu Sant Das ji. Having completed his further studies from St. Johns College Agra, he entered Rajasthan Administrative Service and culminated his work life by making his way into the Indian Administrative Service, as a successful administrator.

Being spiritually inclined right since childhood, after retirement he settled down in Soamibagh,

Agra where he spent the rest of his 30 years totally devoting himself to Satsang, before he left for his divine abode on 24 May, 2019. His uncle Babu Sant Das Maheshwari, an enlightened spiritual being, had made a distinct impact on his life. That was how he too started living his life through the prism of Santmat Radhasoami, Kabir & other saints. Accordingly, on studying how his life had gone through various oscillations it makes us appreciate and absorb some of those reflections that could hold relevance across various timelines.

□□□